Other Ye[...]
by Patricia Reilly [...]
(Illustrated by [...])

YEARLING BOOKS/YOUNG YEARLINGS/YEARLING CLASSICS are designed especially to entertain and enlighten young people. Patricia Reilly Giff, consultant to this series, received her bachelor's degree from Marymount College and a master's degree in history from St. John's University. She holds a Professional Diploma in Reading and a Doctorate of Humane Letters from Hofstra University. She was a teacher and reading consultant for many years, and is the author of numerous books for young readers.

For a complete listing of all Yearling titles, write to
Dell Readers Service,
P.O. Box 1045,
South Holland, IL 60473.

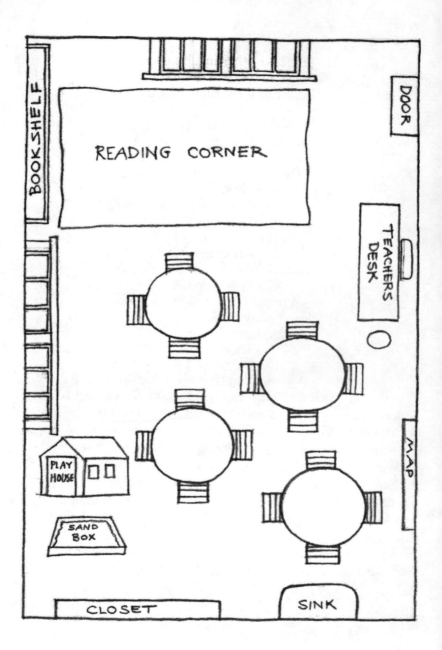

New Kids
6
at the Polk Street School

Stacy Says Good-bye

Patricia Reilly Giff

Illustrated by Blanche Sims

A YOUNG YEARLING BOOK

For Frank Hodge,
with love

Published by
Dell Publishing
a division of
Bantam Doubleday Dell Publishing Group, Inc.
1540 Broadway
New York, New York 10036

ISBN: 0-440-40135-6

Printed in the United States of America

February 1989

10 9 8 7 6

WES

CHAPTER
1

It was morning, almost time for school.

Stacy Arrow picked up her baby picture.

"Bee—you—tee—ful," she sang. "That's me."

She sat on the bed.

She began to bounce.

Her sister Emily came in.

She had toothpaste all over her mouth.

"Why do you have to be so sloppy?"

Emily asked. "This is my room too."

"This is good stuff," Stacy said. "Baby pictures. My baby pictures."

Then she looked around.

Emily was right.

The bedroom was a mess.

Her mother's picture album was on the bed.

Piles of pictures lay on the floor.

So what? She liked a messy bedroom.

Her sister Emily picked up a picture. "Boy, were you fat!" she said.

Stacy smiled. She knew she had been a fat baby.

Her mother always said so.

So did her father.

She put the pictures in a row. "Fat babies are the best."

Emily sat on the floor. She pulled on her socks. "You're prettier now."

Stacy stared at one of the pictures.

Maybe Emily was right.

Her cheeks looked like apples.

Her nose was squashed.

She could hardly see her eyes.

Stacy picked up another picture.

She had to find one that made her look beautiful.

"I have to bring one to school," she told Emily.

Mrs. Arrow came in. "Almost time for school."

"Which picture should I bring?" Stacy asked.

Her mother leaned over. "They're all beautiful. You were a darling baby."

"Pick one," Stacy said.

Her mother pointed her finger.

"Not that one," Emily said. "She looks like a pumpkin."

"I do not," Stacy said.

"Do so," said Emily. "You don't have a hair on your head."

Stacy frowned. She wanted to have the best baby picture in the class.

Mrs. Zachary said they were going to have a special baby bulletin board.

She said she was going to tell them something special too.

"How about this one?" Stacy's mother asked. "Look at this pretty blue dress."

Stacy held up the picture.

She felt herself smiling.

"You're right," she told her mother. "I look beautiful."

She grabbed her jacket.

She went downstairs for her snack bag.

Her mother gave her an envelope for the picture. "Don't lose it."

Stacy held on to the envelope all the way to school.

She didn't even run around in the schoolyard. She stood in line waiting.

She didn't want the picture to get wrinkled.

The beautiful baby picture with the pretty blue dress.

In the classroom everyone was giving pictures to Mrs. Zachary.

Stacy gave hers too.

Mrs. Zachary smiled at her. "Spectacular," she said.

Mrs. Zachary had a nice fat face.

She had nice fat teeth too.

They stuck out a little.

Mrs. Zachary was the best teacher in the whole school.

Stacy opened her snack bag.

She took out the bread crusts she had saved from breakfast.

Mrs. Zachary helped her open the window.

Outside, the birds were waiting to eat.

Mrs. Zachary closed the window quickly. It was cold out.

Stacy sat down in her seat.

She couldn't wait to see everyone's picture.

She couldn't wait to hear Mrs. Zachary's special news.

CHAPTER
2

Everyone in the class had work to do.

They were making *B*'s.

Mrs. Zachary had told them how.

One long line.

One little stomach.

One big stomach.

Easy as one two three, Stacy thought.

She made a bunch of them.

She looked over at Eddie.

His *B*'s were all wrong.

The stomachs were all the same size.

They were wiggly too.

Stacy felt like telling him to start over.

Mrs. Zachary didn't like it when she did that, though.

Stacy turned her paper to the other side.

Maybe she'd make another pile of *B*'s.

She looked around to see if anyone else was finished.

Mrs. Zachary was at the side of the room. She was working on the baby bulletin board. "Don't look," she said. "I want it to be a surprise."

Stacy tried not to look.

It was hard, though.

She took a little peek.

Mrs. Zachary had tacked up pink and blue paper.

She was putting pictures in a row.

Stacy did another *B*.

She smiled to herself.

Her picture was going to be the cutest.

Just then Mrs. Zachary clapped her hands. "Time to look," she said.

Everyone raced over to the side of the room.

They were banging into one another.

"Not so noisy, please," Mrs. Zachary said.

Just then another teacher popped her head into the room.

It was Mrs. Zachary's friend, Ms. Rooney.

Mrs. Zachary went to speak with her.

Stacy looked at the bulletin board.

First she tried to find her picture. She wanted to see if it was the best.

It was there—in the middle.

On top was a picture of a little boy. He was peeking out of a blue blanket.

Adorable.

"Me," said Eddie.

Next was a baby in pink.

She had lots of straight black hair.

Jiwon.

Beautiful.

Stacy looked back at her own picture.

Not so hot.

No. Terrible.

"Look at that one," Annie said. She whistled a little.

Annie was always whistling.

Stacy looked up. It was a baby with big brown eyes. "Cute."

She pointed to her own picture. "What about that one?"

Annie began to laugh.

"Why are you laughing?" Stacy asked.

"That's some fat baby," said Annie.

"Fat is the best," said Stacy.

"Like a little hippopotamus," said Twana.

"A hippopotamus without hair," said Annie.

Stacy didn't answer.

Her face felt hot.

"Which one is yours?" Twana asked.

Stacy went back to her seat.

"The hippopotamus," she said over her shoulder.

Stacy looked toward the door.

She hoped Mrs. Zachary didn't think she was a hippopotamus.

Ms. Rooney was smiling. "Exciting news," she was saying.

Mrs. Zachary shook her head. "I haven't told them yet."

Ms. Rooney laughed. She closed the door behind her.

Stacy hoped she wasn't going to cry. She swallowed hard.

"Is everyone ready?" Mrs. Zachary asked.

"Ready for the news," said A.J.

Mrs. Zachary nodded. "Don't you love the baby pictures?"

The whole class said yes together.

"Here comes my news." Mrs. Zachary took a breath. "I'm going to have a baby too."

Everyone clapped.

They all said oh.

"I knew it all the time," Patty was saying.

Twana yelled, "My mother is going to have a baby in August."

Lucky Twana.

Stacy clicked her teeth.

She wished her mother would have a baby too.

Nothing exciting ever happened at her house.

Mrs. Zachary was smiling. "Just like all the pictures."

"Do you want a boy or a girl?" Jiwon asked.

Mrs. Zachary raised her shoulders in the air.

She looked happy. Her cheeks were pink.

Then she looked at the clock. "Oops. I forgot. It's time for Music."

Everyone rushed to line up.

Everyone but Stacy.

She went slowly.

She had just thought of something.

Something terrible.

What would happen when Mrs. Zachary had the baby?

Suppose she left the Polk Street School?

Suppose she left Stacy's class?

It was the worst thing she could think of.

CHAPTER
3

It was after school.
Stacy had to wait for Emily.
Emily was practicing for a play.
In the hall Stacy hopped on the tiles.
First a brown one.
Then a tan one.
Emily was taking a long time.
Too long.

Stacy hopped back to Mrs. Zachary's room.

She peeked inside.

Mrs. Zachary was still there.

She was straightening her desk drawers.

Stacy wanted to ask the teacher a question

A special question.

She was afraid, though.

She didn't want Mrs. Zachary to give the wrong answer.

Stacy hopped on the tiles again.

Two brown ones.

One tan.

She tried not to step on a crack.

If she stepped on a crack, the teacher might leave.

If she didn't step on a crack, the teacher might stay.

Mrs. Zachary came to the door. "I thought I heard someone," she said.

"I'm waiting for Emily," said Stacy. "I have nothing to do."

"Why don't you sit in the classroom?" Mrs. Zachary asked.

Stacy followed her inside. "I could help you. My mother says I'm a good cleaner."

Mrs. Zachary smiled. "Spectacular."

The teacher pulled a desk drawer out all the way.

She put it on a table.

Stacy looked in the drawer.

Clips had fallen out of a box.

Stars had fallen out of another one.

"I'll put everything back," Stacy said.

She began to put the clips in a cup.

It was nice to be alone with Mrs. Zachary.

Mrs. Zachary was the best teacher in the whole school. Maybe in the whole world.

"I love the baby pictures," said Mrs. Zachary. "Don't you?"

"Not so much."

"Really?" Mrs. Zachary said.

Stacy didn't answer. She kept looking in the desk drawer.

She hoped the teacher didn't remember which picture was hers.

"What a cute baby you were," Mrs. Zachary said.

"I was a hippopotamus." Stacy said it in a low voice. "Fat cheeks—no hair."

Mrs. Zachary laughed.

Stacy dropped a clip into the cup.

She opened her mouth.

Then she closed it again.

"Did you want to say something?" Mrs. Zachary asked.

"I guess not." Stacy sighed. She picked up a blue star.

She put it in a box.

"Take a star," said Mrs. Zachary. "Put it on your collar."

Stacy picked a gold one.

Gold was the best.

She took a breath. She had to ask a question. "How are you going to take care of the class?"

Mrs. Zachary looked over at her. "You mean when I have the baby?"

Stacy nodded.

Mrs. Zachary stood up.

She put her arm around Stacy. "I have to stay home for a while."

"I thought so," Stacy said.

"Another teacher will come," said

Mrs. Zachary. "She'll take care of the class."

"For the rest of the year?" Stacy asked.

Mrs. Zachary nodded.

"Then you won't be our teacher anymore."

Mrs. Zachary shook her head a little.

"I don't want another teacher," Stacy began.

"I know," said Mrs. Zachary. "It makes me sad too." She patted Stacy's shoulder. "You'll love the new teacher in no time."

Just then Emily came to the door. "Time to go home now."

Stacy scooped up the rest of the clips.

She dropped them into the cup.

She knew she wouldn't love the new teacher.

She wouldn't even like her.

CHAPTER

4

It was Tuesday afternoon.

Stacy sat in the kitchen.

A towel was wrapped around her head.

"Are you sure this will turn out?" she asked.

"I hope so," said her mother.

"It better work," said Emily. "You need a perm. Your hair is straight as a stick."

"I guess so," Stacy said. She was worried, though.

She was used to her straight brown hair.

She looked at the perm box on the table.

It had a picture on the front.

A picture of a girl with curly hair.

The girl looked spectacular.

Stacy said it to herself. "Spec-tac-u-lar."

It was Mrs. Zachary's favorite word.

Stacy felt a lump in her throat.

It was hard to swallow.

After tomorrow Mrs. Zachary would be gone.

Her baby was coming soon.

Mrs. Zachary's class wouldn't be Mrs. Zachary's class.

They'd be Mrs. Somebody Else's class.

Stacy had forgotten Mrs. Somebody Else's name.

"You'll look nice for the good-bye party," Emily said.

Stacy felt a lump in her throat. "Don't talk about that."

Her mother took the towel off Stacy's head.

She began to pour stuff over her hair.

It smelled strange. Maybe like seaweed.

Stacy hated it.

It made her nose tingle.

"You'll probably get a wonderful new teacher," her mother said.

"No." Stacy shook her head hard. "She'll be terrible."

"Don't wiggle," said her mother.

"How long is this going to take, anyway?" Stacy asked.

She could feel a drop of water on her neck.

It rolled down her back.

Her sweater was all wet.

"I'm sick of getting this perm," she said. "I'm sick of thinking about a new teacher."

Emily picked up an apple. She bit into it. "Listen, Stacy. A new teacher will be fun. You'll probably do interesting stuff. Different stuff."

"Like what?"

"Like new letters."

Stacy thought about Mrs. Zachary.

She thought about making *B*'s. A line. A little stomach. A big stomach.

The new teacher might not know stuff like that.

Her mother patted her shoulder. "We have to wait five minutes now."

"I can't wait that long," Stacy said.

"Think of how you'll look," said her mother. "Besides, I have something to show you."

"A present?" Stacy asked.

She knew it wasn't a present, though.

The Arrows got presents on birthdays and Christmas—not in between.

Her mother nodded. "A lovely present."

Stacy looked up, surprised.

"Sit still," her mother said. "I'll run upstairs. It's in my closet."

Stacy rubbed at her neck. She wondered what it would be.

A new blouse maybe.

She hoped it wasn't that scribble-scrabble plaid kind.

It wasn't.

It wasn't even a present for her.

It was a present for Mrs. Zachary's new baby.

Stacy looked at the little white suit.

"Stretchies," her mother said.

"Adorable," said Emily.

"Adorable," said Stacy too.

Not so adorable, she thought.

She was sick of Mrs. Zachary's baby.

That was all anybody thought of.

The lump was back in her throat.

She shouldn't be angry at a baby. A poor little baby who wasn't even born.

"I can't stand sitting here anymore," she told her mother.

"Just another minute."

"No," said Stacy. "Not even a second. I'm going to turn into a statue. A seaweed statue."

"All right," her mother said.

Stacy knelt up on the chair.

She leaned over the kitchen sink.

Her mother rinsed off her hair. Then she patted her head with a towel.

"Let me comb it a little," she said.

"Ouch," said Stacy.

Her hair was snarled.

Very snarled.

Her mother could hardly get the comb through it.

"Let me look in the mirror," Stacy said.

"It's a little . . ." her mother began.

"It's kind of . . ." Emily said at the same time.

Stacy went over to the mirror.

She stood up on tiptoe.

Part of her hair was squiggles.

The top part.

The bottom part was straight.

She didn't look one bit like the girl on the box.

No. She looked like a mess.

One big terrible mess.

CHAPTER
5

It was Friday, the day of the party.
Mrs. Zachary's last day.

Stacy marched into the schoolyard.
She put the baby's present down.
She wanted to save her place in line.
"What's that smell?" Robert asked.
Stacy ducked her head.
Her hair was the smell.

She knew it.

She raced across the yard.

What would she do when she had to take off her hat?

Just then the bell rang.

Stacy raced back to the line and picked up the present.

She brushed it off a little.

Mrs. Zachary's class marched inside.

Everyone stopped to look at the baby pictures.

Stacy didn't stop, though.

Who wanted to look at her bald-headed picture?

Being bald wasn't so bad, though.

Not nearly as bad as half squiggles, half straight.

Stacy went to put her jacket away.

She untied her hat strings, but left her hat on.

She went to Mrs. Zachary's desk with her present.

Mrs. Zachary would see it first.

"Aren't you going to take your hat off?" the teacher asked.

"I can't," said Stacy. "My hair is horrible."

"Your hair could never be horrible."

"Squiggles," said Stacy.

Just then Annie came along.

She dropped a blue-and-pink box on top of Stacy's.

"Hey," Stacy said.

Robert dropped a package on top of Annie's.

The ribbon was falling off.

Robert was a messy boy.

Stacy couldn't even see her present anymore.

It was crushed on the bottom.

"Never mind," said Mrs. Zachary. She patted Stacy's shoulder. "Last is the best."

"Why are you wearing a hat?" Annie asked.

"It's cold in here," she said.

"Don't be silly," said Patty. She yanked at Stacy's hat.

Mrs. Zachary shook her head. "Leave Stacy alone."

Stacy sat down at her table.

Today wasn't the same as every other day.

There was no time to sharpen pencils.

No time for Show-and-Tell.

"Number-copying time," said Mrs. Zachary. "Quiet as mice."

Everyone tried to be quiet.

No one talked.

No one banged feet against the tables.

Stacy kept her head down.

She felt as if everyone were looking at her.

Everyone was wondering why she was wearing her green wool hat.

It was itchy.

She reached under the back and scratched a little.

Then she reached for her pencil.

Good thing they had to do 4's.

Fours were easy.

Halfway down.

Run across.

Line from top to bottom.

That's what Mrs. Zachary had told them.

Right now Mrs. Zachary was cleaning everything.

She straightened the library corner.

She dusted the little house.

She threw a skillion things out of her closet.

Great things.

A ball of purple yarn.

An almost new yardstick.

Stacy was glad she was the wastebasket monitor.

She had to empty the basket down the hall.

She'd pull out some good stuff and take it home.

But suppose the principal saw her? He might say, *"Take off your hat."*

Then everyone would see her squiggly-straight hair.

Stacy clicked her teeth.

Maybe Robert would empty the basket today.

"All right," said Mrs. Zachary. "Time for fun."

The class pulled the chairs into a circle.

Mrs. Zachary gave out juice.

She gave out cupcakes too.

Some had pink icing.

Some had blue.

Then the door opened.

"Look who's here," said Mrs. Zachary. She was smiling.

Stacy looked.

She knew just who it was.

The new teacher.

Mrs. Zachary had said she was coming. She had on a dress with flowers all over it.

It was a pretty dress.

It even had a lace collar.

Too bad.

She had a skinny face.

She didn't look one bit like Mrs. Zachary.

She was probably horrible.

Besides, she was staring at Stacy's green wool hat.

CHAPTER
6

Stacy wasn't talking to anyone.

Robert sniffed when he stood next to her.

A.J. kept trying to pull off her hat.

And the new teacher was doing everything wrong.

She had done everything wrong for a week.

Stacy pulled her hat down over her eyebrows.

She watched Mrs. Thomas making 8's on the blackboard.

She was making them in plain white chalk. Not yellow like Mrs. Zachary.

She didn't tell them things like straight line—little stomach—big stomach.

She didn't say down, across, up, and down.

No. The children had to figure it out by themselves.

Terrible.

Mrs. Zachary wouldn't like that one bit.

Stacy made a bunch of wiggly eights.

She looked across at Robert.

Robert's eights were much worse than hers.

She scratched under her hat.

Maybe she should tell the teacher.

Stacy raised her hand.

She wiggled it around.

Mrs. Thomas nodded at her.

"You're not supposed to do that," Stacy said.

The teacher looked surprised. "Do what?"

"Put a white number. It's supposed to be yellow."

Mrs. Thomas thought about it. "I like white," she said.

"Mrs. Zachary liked yellow," said Eddie.

Stacy smiled at him. "That's right."

She stood up.

She wanted the teacher to see her better.

"You're supposed to tell a story about the number too," she said.

"That's what Mrs. Zachary did," said Eddie.

Stacy looked over at Eddie.

Eddie was a good friend.

Up in front Mrs. Thomas was thinking again. "Let's see," she began. "Once upon a time . . ."

Stacy shook her head. "Not that kind of story."

Mrs. Thomas didn't pay any attention. "Once upon a time," she said again, "there was a farmer. In his barn were eight cats . . ."

Stacy tried to get Mrs. Thomas's attention. She shook her head hard.

"The cats had little black dots," said the teacher. "All except one. One poor little—"

"It's supposed to be something like this," said Stacy. "One line, one big stomach—"

"Be quiet," Eddie said. "I want to hear the rest of the story."

Stacy stuck her lip out at Eddie.

He wasn't such a hot friend after all.

"Anyway," said Mrs. Thomas, "this poor cat had to find a way to get some spots for himself."

Stacy took a breath.

She was going to try once more. "You're supposed to do it about the number. Like round circle, round circle. Something like that."

"Be quiet, Stacy," Twana said.

"Yes," said Patty. "This is a great story. I like cats."

"You and that green hat on your head all the time," said Annie.

Stacy looked around.

Even Jiwon was frowning at her.

Stacy slid down into her seat.

She looked out the window.

She hardly listened to the story about the poor cat without spots.

Silly story.

It didn't tell one thing about eights.

Stacy looked over at the wastepaper basket.

It was almost full.

She'd empty it right now.

Let the rest of the class listen to a no-good story about a no-good cat.

Stacy stood up.

She went over to the wastepaper basket.

"Not now," said Mrs. Thomas.

Stacy banged down in her seat.
She hated this new teacher.
She hated everyone.
She even hated Mrs. Zachary for leaving.

CHAPTER
7

It was Thursday, time for gym.

Mr. Bell, the gym teacher, was waiting outside.

He blew his whistle. "Today we'll have a relay race."

Stacy pulled up her socks.

She watched the rest of the class.

Half of them lined up next to the tree.

"You're the Stars," Mr. Bell told them.

The other half lined up next to the wall.

"You can be the Stripes," he said.

Stacy tried to think.

Twana was a Star.

Stacy didn't want to be on Twana's side.

She was still angry with Twana.

Twana had told her to be quiet.

Stacy didn't want to be a Stripe either.

Annie was a Stripe.

Annie had been fresh about her green hat.

Stacy took a breath.

She'd stand behind Patty.

It was on the Stars' side—but three ahead of Twana.

Patty was a great girl. Even Mrs. Zachary always said so.

Stacy closed her eyes for a minute.

She didn't want to think about Mrs. Zachary.

Stacy pushed into the Stars' line—behind Patty.

"Hey," said Patty. She made a fresh face. "Stop stepping all over me."

"Who wants to step on you?" Stacy said. "Peanut-butter brain."

She gave Patty a little shove.

Mr. Bell saw her. "Get with it, Stacy," he said.

Mr. Bell gave each of the line leaders a ball.

"Run across the yard with it," he said. "Run back again. Give the ball to the next person."

Everyone was jumping up and down.

A.J. and Eddie raced across the yard.

"Come on, A.J.," yelled the Stars.

"Come on, Eddie," yelled the Stripes.

"Come on, Eddie," Stacy said too. She said it in a little voice.

Eddie had given her a cookie at snack time.

"Are you crazy?" Patty said. "You're yelling for the wrong side."

Eddie and A.J. were back in a flash.

The next two started.

The Stripe line bunched up watching.

Then it was Patty's turn.

Patty ran fast.

She was pulling ahead of the Stars.

Stacy waited to grab the ball.

She put out one foot to get ready.

Patty tossed her the ball.

Stacy caught it and ran.

She went as fast as she could.

Let old whistling Annie see how good she was.

Let mean Twana see she was the best.
The wind blew against her face.

Halfway across the yard was a crack in the cement.

She hopped over it.

Crash.

She went down on her knee.

The ball bounced away from her.

She had to chase all over to get it.

Her knee was scraped.

Nobody cared, though. They kept yelling, "Hurry."

Stacy limped back to the line. She gave the ball to Jiwon.

Patty clicked her teeth at her.

Twana made a face.

The Stars were jumping up and down.

"I have to go to the girls' room," Stacy told Mr. Bell.

She walked across the yard.

Her knee was stinging.

There was a little hole in her jeans.

She opened the big brown doors.

Mrs. Thomas was coming out of the teachers' room.

She had a white envelope in her hand.

"Stacy Arrow," she said. "You're just the person I want to see."

CHAPTER
8

Stacy was sitting in her seat.

She was waiting for the rest of the class.

They'd be back from gym any minute.

Wait till they saw her.

She wasn't wearing her green hat any-more.

Her green hat was in the closet. It was tucked in the sleeve of her jacket.

"Right where it should be," Mrs. Thomas had said.

Stacy raised her hand.

She felt the top of her head.

Mrs. Thomas had combed her hair.

The teacher said she didn't mind squiggles one bit.

Just then the class marched in.

"Hey," said Patty. "Where's your hat?"

Jiwon smiled. "Now you look like Stacy again."

"Almost," said A.J. "Now she has some curls."

"Put your coats away quickly," said Mrs. Thomas. "I have something to show you."

"Something exciting," said Stacy.

Everyone rushed to the closet.

Then they went up to Mrs. Thomas's desk.

Stacy went too.

She felt herself smiling.

Mrs. Thomas opened the envelope again.

"Guess who was just here, boys and girls?" she asked.

"The President," said Eddie.

Stacy laughed. She felt like jumping up and down.

"Not the President," said Mrs. Thomas.

"How about a movie star?" said Patty.

Stacy shook her head.

She put her hands over her mouth.

It was hard not to tell.

"One more guess," said Mrs. Thomas.

"I give up right now," said Annie.

"Me too," said Jiwon.

"Mrs. Zachary," yelled Twana.

Stacy took her hand off her mouth. "Almost," she said.

Everyone looked at her.

"Go ahead, Stacy," said Mrs. Thomas. "Tell the class."

"It was Mr. Zachary," said Stacy. "Look what he brought."

Mrs. Thomas pulled a picture out of the envelope.

"It's a baby," said Twana.

Everyone looked over to see better.

"Not just a baby," said Stacy. "It's Mrs. Zachary's baby."

"Beautiful," said Twana.

"Gorgeous," said Patty.

"Spectacular," said Jiwon.

"She was just one hour old when this picture was taken," said Mrs. Thomas. "Mrs. Zachary wanted you to see her right away."

"What's her name?" A.J. asked.

"Megan," said Stacy. "Megan Elizabeth."

"Hey," Twana said. She looked at the bulletin board.

Then she looked back at the picture of Megan Elizabeth.

Her mouth was open.

Mrs. Thomas winked at Stacy.

Stacy tried to wink back.

It was hard, though.

She had to use both eyes.

"Look," said Twana.

Jiwon looked at the bulletin board too. "The baby looks just like . . ."

A.J. leaned over. "Just like Stacy."

"Stacy Arrow," said Eddie.

Everyone raced to the side of the room.

They looked at Stacy's picture.

"Fat," said Stacy, smiling.

"That's the way babies are supposed to look," said Mrs. Thomas.

"Like a hippopotamus," said Stacy.

"A cute one," said Twana.

"An adorable one," said Jiwon.

"Wait," said Mrs. Thomas. "You haven't heard the rest."

Everyone raced back to Mrs. Thomas's desk.

"There's something written on the back of the picture," Mrs. Thomas said.

She turned it over.

"What does it say?" Annie asked.

Stacy closed her eyes.

She felt warm inside.

Wonderful.

"It says:

Here is Megan Elizabeth. Isn't she beautiful? Doesn't she look like Stacy? If Stacy takes her hat off, you'll see how Megan may look when she gets hair! I hope she's as nice as Stacy, don't you?"

Everyone looked at Stacy.

"Not bad," said A.J.

"Pretty good," said Annie. "Especially without that hat."

They all laughed.

Mrs. Thomas was smiling too. "It's time to learn some nines," she said.

Stacy rushed back to her seat. She felt good inside. Great.

She didn't mind her squiggle hair one bit.

She hoped Mrs. Thomas would tell a story.

Maybe it would be about cats. Nine cats and a bunch of black spots.

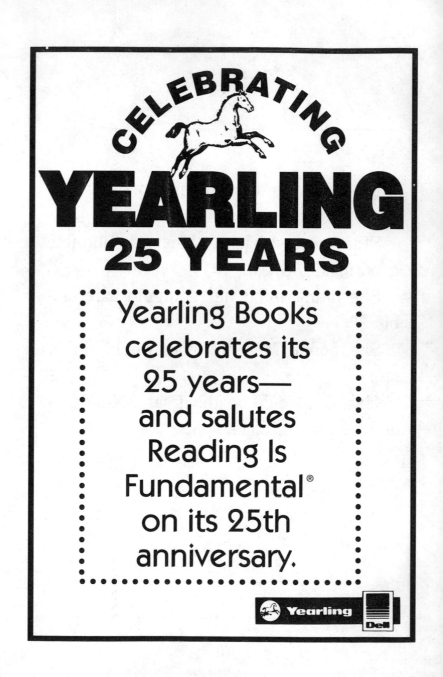